The Magical Graggle

'Lost in the Woods'

Amanda Lambert

Dedication

For Aaliyah and Mya

For Warren, whom I could not have done this without

In Evergreen Wood not too far away,

There lived a magical Graggle who had lost his way.

He searched and searched around,

But nothing familiar could be found.

The Graggle looked low, the Graggle looked high.

The Graggle felt lonely, he wanted to cry.

He sat on a rock and cried a small tear.

"How will I ever get out of here?"

"Wait! I am magical!" The Graggle realised,

And he jumped from the rock and wiped his eyes.

But instead of looking around for clues.

The Graggle thought of a spell he could use!

He wriggled his fingers, he wriggled his toes,

He shook his bottom and twitched his nose.

"Take me up high so I can see

which way to go that is best for me".

Just then an eagle came out of the sky,

Grabbed the Graggle and took him up **high!**

The Graggle was being flown all around,

The Graggle was very far from the ground.

"Oh no! That is not what I wanted I didn't do well.

I better think quickly and cast another spell!"

He wriggled his fingers, he wriggled his toes,
He shook his bottom and twitched his nose.

"Let me down now, I was wrong, I lied. Let me down now so I can be inside".

With that the eagle opened his claws,

And dropped the Graggle inside a crocodile's **jaws!**

The Graggle looked around in the dark; he was inside the Crocodile's tummy!

The Graggle wanted to get out, but the Crocodile thought he was yummy!

"Oh no! That is not what I wanted I didn't do well.

I better think quickly and cast another spell!"

He wriggled his fingers, he wriggled his toes,

He shook his bottom and twitched his nose.

"Get me out of this crocodile tummy!

Get me out, get me out, I don't want to be yummy!"

Just then the Crocodile let out an enormous sneeze.

The Graggle flew out and got stuck in the **trees!**

The Graggle felt cross, the Graggle felt sad.

The Graggle was starting to feel quite mad!

"Oh no! That is not what I wanted I didn't do well.

I better think quickly and cast another spell!"

He wriggled his fingers, he wriggled his toes,

He shook his bottom and twitched his nose.

But as the Graggle hung upside down by his toes,

He suddenly fell off and bumped his **nose!**

The Graggle felt cross, the Graggle felt bad.

His spells had not worked and now he was sad.

"NO MORE SPELLS!" Shouted the Graggle with a frown.

So, he took a deep breath and tried to calm down.

Now the Graggle was calmer he began to feel good.

He thought about how to find his way in this wood.

The Graggle stood up and looked all around,

The Graggle was surprised at what he had found.

The Graggle called out, "Look, this tree is near mine!"

"This apple tree is the one I go past all the time!"

The Graggle walked further until he got back to his hole.

The tiring day had certainly taken its toll.

The Graggle lay his head and said goodnight to the moon.

He felt that he would have another adventure quite soon.

About the Author

Amanda is a Reception class teacher who has always had a passion for children's books. She has a collection of favourite children's stories which she has referred to throughout her career and whilst her own children were growing up. Amanda used to write stories for her own children when they were young and spend many hours re-reading their favourite stories to them. Amanda believes that sharing stories together is a wonderful way to encourage imagination, passion and creativity in growing minds.

Printed in Great Britain
by Amazon

34357551R00016